Questions and Answers: Countries

Greece

A Question and Answer Book

by Kremena Spengler

Consultant:
Theofanis G. Stavrou
Professor of History
Director, Modern Greek Studies
University of Minnesota, Minneapolis, Minnesota

Capstone
press

Mankato, Minnesota

Fact Finders is published by Capstone Press
151 Good Counsel Drive, P.O. Box 669, Mankato, Minnesota 56002.
www.capstonepress.com

Library of Congress Cataloging-in-Publication Data
Spengler, Kremena.
    Greece : a question and answer book / by Kremena Spengler.
    p. cm.—(Fact finders. Questions and answers. Countries)
    Includes bibliographical references and index.
    ISBN–13: 978–0–7368–6769–6 (hardcover)
    ISBN–10: 0–7368–6769–4 (hardcover)
    1. Greece—Miscellanea—Juvenile literature. I. Title. II. Series.
DF717.S68 2007
949.5—dc22   2006028501

Summary: Describes the geography, history, economy, and culture of Greece in a
    question-and-answer format.

Editorial Credits
Silver Editions, editorial, design, photo research and production; Kia Adams, set designer;
    Maps.com, cartographer

Photo Credits
Alamy/IML Image Group Ltd, 23: terry harris just greece photo library, 27
AP/Wide World Photos/Aris Messinis, 19
The Bridgeman Art Library/Greek School, (19th Century), 7
Capstone Press Archives, 29 (money)
Corbis/Kevin Schafer, 21; Owen Franken, 17, 25; Richard Klune, 15
Getty Images Inc./AFP/Aris Messinis, 9; Stone/Will & Deni McIntyre, cover (foreground);
    Taxi/Vega, 1
The Image Works/Visum/Ralf Niemzig, 13
Medio Images, cover (background), 4, 11
One Mile Up, Inc. 29 (flag)

1 2 3 4 5 6 12 11 10 09 08 07

Table of Contents

Features

Where is Greece?

Greece is in southeastern Europe at the tip of the Balkan **Peninsula**. More than 2,000 islands are also part of Greece. Some of them are large, but others are more like big rocks. All of Greece combined is a bit smaller than the U.S. state of Alabama.

Warm air picks up water from the seas around Greece. This moist air brings mild weather to most of the country. Only the tallest mountains receive snow in winter.

Many towns in Greece spread out over coastal hillsides.

Map of Greece

Legend

✪	Capital
●	City
▲	Mountain Peak
⛰	Mountain Range

BULGARIA

MACEDONIA

ALBANIA

●Thessaloníki

Mount Olympus ▲
●Lárisa
●Vólos

Pindus Mountains

Aegean Sea

TURKEY

●Khalkís

✪**Athens**

Corinth Canal

Ionian Sea

Peloponnesus Peninsula

G R E E C E

Mediterranean Sea

Sea of Crete

Rhodes

●Iráklion
Crete

Scale
0   50   100 Miles
0   50   100 Kilometers

Mountains and rocky hills cover most of Greece. The Pindus Mountains stretch from north to south. Mountains in the south form walls around lowlands, valleys, and beaches. The highest point in Greece is Mount Olympus.

5

When did Greece become a country?

Greece became a country in 1828 after ending Turkish rule. In ancient times, Greece was made up of **city-states**. Then it became an empire that ruled much of the ancient world.

The Greeks had no single, strong army. About 2,100 years ago, the Roman Empire took over Greece. Then in 1453, Greece came under Turkish rule. Almost 400 years later, the Greeks fought and won their freedom from the Turks.

Fact!

Greece is known as the birthplace of Western civilization because of its lasting ideas in philosophy and government.

The cities of Athens and Sparta fought one another often in ancient Greece. In this painting, Spartan ships attack Piraeus, a port city close to Athens.

Then the Greeks faced an important question. Should they have a king or become a **republic** and vote for their leaders? Greece had a king until 1974. Then the people decided to become a republic.

What type of government does Greece have?

Greece is a **democratic** republic. Elections take place every four years. All Greeks who are age 18 or older must vote.

The 300 members of **parliament** make the country's laws. Unlike the U.S. Congress, Greece's parliament has only one house. Parliament elects a president to lead the country. The president serves for up to two five-year terms. The president also selects a **prime minister**.

Fact!

Greeks invented the democratic form of government more than 2,400 years ago. The word democracy comes from the Greek words for "rule of the people."

Representatives in Greece's parliament meet to decide on the country's laws.

The prime minister is the leader of the political party that won the most recent election. He runs the government and chooses a **cabinet** to help him. Cabinet members run government departments.

As in the United States, the Greek government has a **judicial** branch. Courts decide how to apply the country's laws.

What kind of housing does Greece have?

Many houses in Greece are built of stone or **stucco** with red tiled roofs. Vines and colorful flowers often grow in the courtyards.

Weather affects the style of houses. Because Greece gets a lot of sunshine, many houses are painted white. This color reflects the bright sun and keeps the inside cool.

Where do people live in Greece?

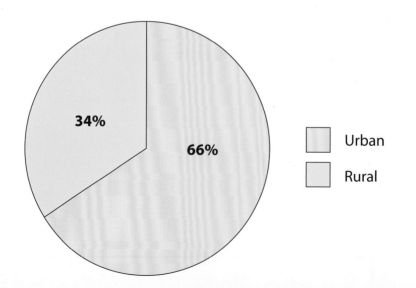

34%

66%

Urban

Rural

The rich colors on many Greek houses represent the land, sky, and sea.

In larger cities, some people live in houses and others live in apartments. Apartments generally cost less than houses. Many apartments have balconies for people to enjoy the sunshine and warm weather.

What are Greece's forms of transportation?

The roads and railroads in Greece are modern. Many people rely on highways for their travel. Buses and trains run regularly between cities and towns in the countryside.

Greek cities also have public transportation. In Athens, for example, people can take city buses, electric trolley buses, or other public vehicles. Athens also has a new, modern subway.

Fact!

The Corinth Canal was built in the 1800s. It separates central Greece from southern Greece. Ships use the canal as a shortcut for traveling around the peninsula.

Προς Δάφνη
To Dafni

A subway train arrives in a modern underground station in Athens.

The Athens Airport is the country's most modern airport. It was specially built for the 2004 Olympic Games.

Because Greece has many islands, sea travel is common. Ferry boats carry passengers between coastal towns and islands.

What are Greece's major industries?

Greece has a large service industry. Each year, millions of tourists visit the country's ancient ruins. They can see temples built in honor of Greek gods and goddesses. Many tourists also enjoy relaxing on the beautiful beaches. To meet the needs of tourists, Greeks run many hotels, restaurants, ferryboats, and other service businesses.

What does Greece import and export?

Imports	Exports
basic manufactured goods	manufactured goods
food and animals	food and drinks
crude oil	petroleum products
chemicals	cement
machinery	chemicals
transport equipment	

A fisherman in the coastal town of Fiskardo inspects his fishing nets.

Greeks have lived by the sea for thousands of years. The shipping and fishing industries remain strong. Many people still operate family fishing boats.

Farmers in Greece grow olives, grapes, wheat, and cotton. These crops grow well in the warm climate.

What is school like in Greece?

In Greece, children must go to school from ages 6 to 15. Elementary school lasts six years. Middle school lasts three years, and high school usually takes three years. Although students do not have to attend high school, most of them do.

Fact!

The Greek thinkers Socrates, Aristotle, and Plato are still considered to be three of the greatest teachers of all time.

Public schools in Greece are free for students.

Greece has several kinds of middle and high schools. Most teach basic subjects such as math and reading. Some also have classes such as music or religion. Some high schools train students for technical work or other jobs. After high school, many students attend a university or a technical college.

What are Greece's favorite sports and games?

Soccer is the most popular sport in Greece. Many Greeks will stop any other activity to watch the national team. Major cities have teams that play each other on Sundays.

Because Greece is on the sea, many people enjoy water sports. Parents often teach children to fish and swim at an early age. Sailing, rowing, and diving are also common.

Fact!

The first marathon took place in ancient Greece. About 2,500 years ago, a runner raced to Athens with news of Greece's victory over Persia in the Battle of Marathon. He ran 26 miles (41. 8 kilometers).

Greek soccer players battle for the ball during a match in Athens.

    The Olympic Games began in ancient Greece almost 2,800 years ago. Athens hosted the first modern Olympics in 1896. It also hosted the Olympics in 2004. The Olympic Games continue to attract the world's best athletes.

What are the traditional art forms in Greece?

Greece is known around the world for its **architecture**. Ancient Greeks built many temples, theaters, and palaces. Large columns hold up figures and scenes from mythology carved in stone.

Greeks are proud of their folk arts. Some artists are skilled in weaving and needlework. Many people enjoy traditional folk dances.

Fact!

Greek artists were the first to make their drawings and sculptures look as much like life as possible.

Many ancient Greek theaters were built so well that even people in the top rows could hear every sound.

The first European written works of lasting value came from Greece. Homer created two long poems, the *Iliad* and the *Odyssey*. Writers in ancient Greece wrote plays that included both comedy and tragedy. You can still see these plays on stage today.

What holidays do people in Greece celebrate?

Most Greeks celebrate Christian holidays through the Greek Orthodox Church. Their biggest holiday is Easter. On the night before Easter Sunday, all church lights go out at midnight. One by one, people light candles. As they head home, the candles twinkle in the night.

What other holidays do people in Greece celebrate?

New Year's Day
Epiphany
Independence Day
Mayday (Labor Day)
Holy Spirit Day
Assumption of Mary
Ochi Day
Christmas Day

Easter is an important holiday in the Greek Orthodox Church. Many people take part in elaborate ceremonies.

Each Greek village has a **patron saint**. The people honor their saint each year with a festival. People named after the saint also celebrate that day. Name days are more important than birthdays.

What are the traditional foods of Greece?

Greeks use many local ingredients in their cooking. Sheep and goats raised in the mountains provide meat. People make soft, white feta (FEH-tah) cheese from the milk of these animals. The seas around Greece are a great source of fish.

Greeks also serve locally grown fruits and vegetables in their meals. Tomatoes and olives are common in Greek salads. The Greeks use olive oil to prepare all kinds of foods. Grapes, peaches, and watermelons often appear on the dessert menu.

Fact!

Since ancient times, Greeks have served small helpings of fruits and nuts called "spoon sweets" to welcome their guests to a meal.

No Greek salad would be complete without tomatoes, olives, and feta cheese.

Moussaka (moo-sah-KAH) and dolmades (dol-MAH-thehs) are favorite Greek dishes. Ground meat, eggplant, and sauces are baked together to make moussaka. Dolmades are grape leaves stuffed with ground meat or rice.

What is family life like in Greece?

Greeks value their families a great deal. It is common for grandparents, parents, and children to live together in one place. People often care for their older parents in the family home. Families often visit each other for meals, long talks about the news, or games.

What are the ethnic backgrounds of people in Greece?

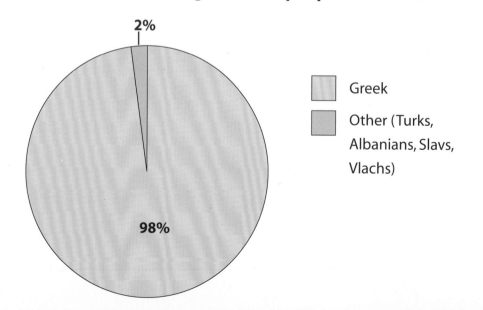

2%

98%

Greek

Other (Turks, Albanians, Slavs, Vlachs)

Greek weddings are huge and important events that bring many friends and family members together.

Greeks highly value their friends, too. Traditionally, Greeks keep close ties with the best man and maid of honor at their weddings. This couple later becomes godparents to the family's children. The extended family celebrates many occasions together.

Greece Fast Facts

Official name:

Hellenic Republic

Population:

10,668,000 people

Land area:

50,471 square miles
(130,800 square kilometers)

Capital city:

Athens

Average annual precipitation (Athens):

16 inches (40.6 centimeters)

Languages:

Greek, English, French

Average January temperature (Athens):

50 degrees Fahrenheit
(10 degrees Celsius)

Natural resources:

bauxite, lignite, magnesite, petroleum, marble

Average July temperature (Athens):

82 degrees Fahrenheit
(28 degrees Celsius)

Religions:

Greek Orthodox	98%
Muslim	1.3%
Other	0.7%

Money and Flag

Money:

Greece's money is the euro. In 2006, 1 U.S. dollar equaled .78 euro. One Canadian dollar equaled .71 euro.

Flag:

Greece's flag has nine equal stripes of blue and white. The stripes stand for the nine syllables of the Greek phrase "freedom or death." A blue square with a white cross is in the top left corner of the flag. The cross stands for the country's Greek Orthodox faith.

Learn to Speak Greek

Most people in Greece speak Greek. It is the official language. Learn to speak some Greek words and phrases below.

English	Greek	Pronunciation
yes	ne	(NEH)
no	ohi	(O-hee)
excuse me	signomi	(sig-NO-mee)
please	parakalo	(pah-rah-kah-LO)
thank you	efharisto	(ef-hah-ree-STOH)
I'm sorry	Lipame	(lee-PAH-mee)
good morning/good day	kalimera	(kah-lee-MEH-rah)
good evening	kalispera	(kah-lee-SPEH-rah)

Glossary

architecture (AHR-ki-tekt-chuhr)—the designing of buildings

cabinet (KA-bi-net)—a group of government ministers that help run a country

city-state (SI-tee STAYT)—a self-governing community including a town and its surrounding territory

democratic (deh-maw-KRA-tic)—having a kind of government in which citizens vote for their leaders

judicial (joo-DISH-uhl)—to do with the branch of government that explains and interprets the laws

parliament (PAR-luh-ment)—the group of people who have been elected to make laws in some countries

patron saint (PAY-truhn SAYNT)—a saint in the church to whom a person or place is dedicated

peninsula (puh-NIN-suh-luh)—a piece of land that is surrounded by water on three sides

prime minister (PRIME MIN-uh-ster)—the person in charge of a government in some countries

republic (ree-PUHB-lik)—a government run by elected officials

stucco (STUH-koh)—a kind of plaster used on walls and ceilings

Internet Sites

FactHound offers a safe, fun way to find Internet sites related to this book. All of the sites on FactHound have been researched by our staff.

Here's how:
1. Visit *www.facthound.com*
2. Choose your grade level.
3. Type in this book ID **0736867694** for age-appropriate sites. You may also browse subjects by clicking on letters, or by clicking on pictures and words.
4. Click on the **Fetch It** button.

FactHound will fetch the best sites for you!

Read More

Augustin, Byron, and Rebecca Augustin. *Greece.* A to Z. New York: Children's Press, 2005.

Etingoff, Kim. *Greece.* European Union. Philadelphia: Mason Crest, 2006.

Nardo, Don. *Ancient Greece.* The Greenhaven Encyclopedia of. San Diego: Greenhaven Press, 2006.

Shahrukh, Husain. *Greece.* Stories from Ancient Civilizations. North Mankato, Minn.: Smart Apple Media, 2005.

Index